UNINVITED GUESTS

The fiendish fun continues at
www.screamstreet.com

For my dad,
Brian Donbavand

First published 2016 by Walker Books Ltd
87 Vauxhall Walk, London SE11 5HJ

2 4 6 8 10 9 7 5 3 1

© 2016 Coolabi Productions Limited
Based on the Scream Street series of books by Tommy Donbavand

Based on the scripts "Haunted House" by Giles Pilbrow and Ben Ward and "Wolf Gang" by Giles Pilbrow.

This book has been typeset in Bembo Educational

Printed and bound in Great Britain by Clays Ltd, St Ives plc

British Library Cataloguing in Publication Data: a catalogue record for this book is available from the British Library

ISBN 978-1-4063-6784-3
www.walker.co.uk

UNINVITED GUESTS

Tommy Donbavand

WALKER
ENTERTAINMENT

LUKE WATSON

With a troublesome taste for adventure, Luke is much like any other teenage boy – oh, except for the fact that he's also a werewolf. If he gets upset, stay well clear of him!

CLEO FARR

Cleo is a feisty teen mummy who's been in Scream Street for centuries. She's used that time to become an expert at martial arts, which comes in handy rather often.

RESUS NEGATIVE

Resus is the sarcastic son of two vampires. But he didn't get the vampire gene himself, so there's no drinking blood or turning into a bat for him – much to his disappointment.

DIG

Dig is a lovable, half-dead dog. He has a skeletal rear end, which is unfortunate, as he is quite fond of chewing on bones. He also does his very best to live up to his name.

MIKE WATSON

Luke's dad really doesn't want to be In Scream Street. He's easily frightened, and his screams are regularly heard echoing around town.

SUE WATSON

Sue does her best to keep her son, Luke, on the straight and narrow, while also trying to get her husband to pull himself together.

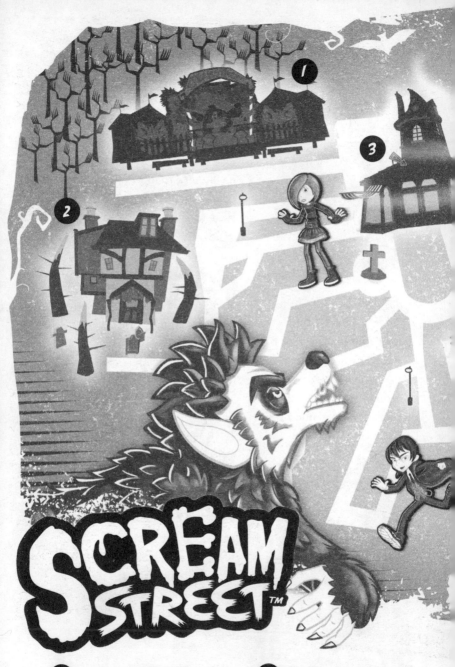

SCREAM STREET™

1 THE GHOST TRAIN   3 EEFA'S EMPORIUM

2 HAUNTED HOUSE   4 SNEER HALL

WHERE BEING A FREAK IS TOTALLY NORMAL...

5 CLEO'S HOUSE

6 THE GRAVEYARD

1 RESUS'S AND LUKE'S HOUSES

CONTENTS

Haunted House

Wolf Gang

HAUNTED HOUSE

Chapter One

THE HOUSE

The werewolf's powerful legs pounded as Luke picked up speed. Large feet covered with thick fur stomped down the dense, decaying vegetation that covered the woodland floor. Ah, there was nothing like taking his werewolf legs out for a run! With every stride, dead trees shot past in an impossible blur.

Ahead lay a river. Just an innocent, slow-moving body of water at first glance, but Luke knew it contained fish that could strip flesh from bone in seconds with their razor-sharp teeth. Anyone - or anything - foolish enough to dip a toe into the ice-cold stream would instantly pay the price.

When he reached the bank, Luke used all the power of his werewolf legs to leap into the air. He stretched his arms towards a thick branch over-hanging the river, managing somehow to grip the black, rotting wood and using his momentum to carry himself forward. Luke prayed the branch would hold... And it did.

He landed hard on the far side of the river, one furry heel splashing into the water's edge and causing a flurry of activity as its deadly occupants fought for a taste of flesh. But by the time the fish reached the bank, fangs snapping, the potential meal was already gone.

Just one obstacle left - the enormous fallen tree that had outwitted Luke on more than one early morning workout. Today, however, the run was not going to end here. Today, he would continue on, deeper into the unexplored part of the woods.

Timing each stride carefully, Luke jumped as he reached the immovable tree trunk, both feet landing squarely on the rough bark. His werewolf knees took over, bending into a crouch then – muscles screaming with the effort – propelling him up into the air and over into a perfect somersault.

This time, he would land safely. This time, the run would continue.

"*Yes!*"

Then he skidded and slammed, face first, into a solid brick wall and fell to the ground with an embarrassing *crump*!

"Ow!" cried Luke Watson, rubbing his nose as his partial werewolf transformation began to reverse. He pulled his fingers away and saw they were smudged with blood.

Untangling his now human legs, he climbed to his feet and examined the wall that had stopped him in its tracks. He ran his hand over the peeling purple paint, feeling the rough brickwork underneath.

"Who on earth put this house here?" he asked out loud.

Mike Watson opened the oven and grinned as the aroma of roasting chicken wafted towards him. Memories of life before Scream Street came flooding back: Sunday dinner with music playing in the background – a proper vinyl record, of course. Then a quick snooze in front of the TV while his wife did the dishes and Luke finished his homework.

Today was going to be a good day!

"Mmm! Delicious!" he declared, sliding the chicken from the oven shelf and carrying it to the dining table to sit beside a mound of roast potatoes and a bowl of steaming vegetables.

Sue, his wife, joined him at the table, opening a bottle of ice-cold lemonade.

No, strike that, Mike thought. Today was going to be a *great* day!

He had just picked up the carving knife and was holding it above the roast when Luke skidded to a stop in the doorway. He was out of breath, and wiping his still-bloody fingers on the back of his jeans.

"Mum! Dad!" he cried. "They've put up another house in the woods! Must be new arrivals. Can I go over to say hello?"

"Of course," said his mum, sliding the cork back into the lemonade bottle before she had poured a single drop. "We should all go."

Mike sat down heavily at the table, his dream of a great day already starting to unravel. "No, no, no!" he cried, waving his hands. "I have no desire whatsoever to find out what manner of monster has moved in down the road."

He took the bottle of lemonade from his wife and pulled out the cork again.

"I am about to tuck into a nice, ordinary Sunday lunch. Please just let me enjoy it."

Silence fell over the dining room.

Mike sighed happily. He'd done it. He'd stood his ground and won. Today wasn't going to be about mad monsters and crazy creatures. Today was going to be about normal things, things like lemonade, steaming carrots and roast chicken.

Reaching out, he pulled a leg from the cooked bird in the centre of the table and held it under his nose, taking a long sniff. This was going to be the best meal he'd had in—

Suddenly, the roast chicken jumped up to stand in its serving tray and glare at him. No, thought Mike. That can't be right! The chicken hasn't got a face! How can it be glaring at me?

Before Mike could continue with this train of thought, the chicken lunged forward and snatched its recently detached leg from his grip. Then it turned, leapt down from the dinner table,

17

and hopped out the door.

The Watson family watched it leave in silence. Then, as they heard the front door slam, Luke turned back to his parents and shrugged.

"Looks like the chicken's off," he said.

Mike clamped a hand over his mouth and dashed for the bathroom.

Thirty minutes later, Luke was standing outside the new house in the woods with Resus Negative and Cleo Farr. Since his family had moved to Scream Street, Luke had taken part in numerous adventures with his new friends – adventures that had seen the vampire and Egyptian mummy come to his rescue just as many times as he'd been there for them. Now the trio was inseparable, especially on days like today, when there was somewhere new and exciting to explore.

"See!" said Luke. "It looks like a normal, old haunted house."

"And you reckon it just appeared out of nowhere?" asked Cleo.

"Well, it wasn't here yesterday," said Luke. "I've gone running in the woods every day for weeks. I would have noticed if there'd been a great big house in the way."

Resus stepped back to take in the front of the house all at once. "I've never heard of an entire house just appearing overnight before."

Luke shrugged. "Maybe it was an emergency relocation for someone by G.H.O.U.L.?" The Movers from the Government Housing of Unusual Lifeforms (G.H.O.U.L.) had relocated Luke's own family to Scream Street when his werewolf identity became known.

"So, who do you think lives here?" asked Resus.

"Hmmm," mused Cleo. "It's not fancy enough to be vampires. Not gross enough to be bogeymen. And not stinky enough to be werewolves."

Luke spun to face her. "Oi!"

Cleo stuck out her tongue, then thrust her hands onto her hips. "You think we don't know you've been out running with those werewolf legs?" she demanded. "You pass my house on your way home — and let me tell you, sweat really sticks to werewolf fur!"

Resus began to giggle. "What?" he cried, as Luke glared at him. "Cleo's right! You don't half pong when you've been exercising with those legs. My mum was convinced her Great-Uncle Wilhelm had turned up for a visit yesterday — and he's been undead for two hundred years!"

Despite his embarrassment, Luke allowed himself a smile. "All right," he said. "I'll make sure I give the legs a wash next time."

"You'd better," said Cleo. "'Cos right now, you smell like ... roast chicken?"

"That's not me!" said Luke. "That's my dad's Sunday dinner! Here it comes now."

The trio watched as the chicken came bounding through the woods, being chased by a dog who was cute and hairy at the front, but whose back end was nothing but bones.

"Dig!" said Luke, sternly. "Leave the poor bird alone!"

Dig ignored Luke and began to growl at the chicken. The roast lunch trembled, dropping the leg it had rescued from Luke's dad. With a triumphant yelp, Dig darted forward, snatched up the tasty treat and swallowed it in one gulp — only for the leg to reappear in one piece at Dig's other end.

Buoyed by this stroke of luck, the chicken

reclaimed its leg and hopped away, Dig once more in pursuit.

Cleo turned her attention back to the old house. "Do you reckon they have kids?" she asked.

"There's only one way to find out," said Luke, taking a step forward.

"Do we have to?" sighed Resus.

Luke grabbed the large metal knocker, which was shaped like a house, and hammered it against the wood of the door. The trio stood silently for a moment as the knocks echoed away inside the building.

"OK," said Resus cheerfully. "There's nobody in. Let's go home!"

But just as the vampire turned to leave, the front door opened slightly with a *crrreeeaaakkkkk*!

"Oh, come on, Resus," said Luke. "The door's open. We might as well go in!"

Resus folded his arms and stayed rooted to the spot. Despite being born to vampire parents, Resus was a normal boy. He tried to hide this by dyeing his hair black and wearing false nails and fangs, but his reflection could be seen wherever there was a reflective surface. The one extra-ordinary thing about him was his extreme level of caution.

"Come on," urged Luke. "Where's your sense of adventure?"

"It went *on* an adventure and died!" snapped Resus. "Horribly! Like we almost did the last time you said, 'Oh, the door's open, we might as well go in!'"

The roast chicken hopped past the vampire's feet and up onto a nearby dustbin. Dig continued to sniff around on the ground, trying to pick up its trail.

"Anyway," continued Resus, "we can't just walk into someone's house!"

But it was too late. Luke was already in the hallway, Cleo at his heels.

"Hello?" Luke called.

Resus groaned. "You two never listen to me!"

"Oh, don't be such a big wuss!" teased Cleo from the doorway.

"It's all right for you, Little Miss 'I'll be fine, my internal organs are safe in a fridge'," Resus said.

Cleo scowled. While it was true that the organs she'd had removed when she was mummified were now kept safe in plastic tubs in the refrigerator at home, she could still be injured … or worse.

"Suit yourself," she grumbled, following Luke inside.

Resus stood his ground, determined not to move. Then an owl hooted loudly in the trees above and made him jump.

"I just *know* I'm going to regret this!" Resus muttered as he hurried into the old house behind his friends.

The door slammed shut behind them.

Chapter Two

THE ROOM

Luke, Resus and Cleo stood in the hallway of the empty house and stared at the mess. The carpets were old and stained, the paintwork on the banisters leading to the upper floor was chipped, and aged stripy-green wallpaper was peeling from the walls.

Hanging at irregular intervals all around the hallway were pictures of other houses. Some looked like the kind of child's drawing that usually finds a home on the front of a

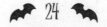

family refrigerator, while others were delicate oil paintings in golden frames. No two houses looked the same.

Luke dipped a toe into a sticky puddle in front of them. "Whoever built this place really put the work in," he said. "But it looks as though it's been empty for decades."

"It smells bad too," said Cleo, pulling her bandages up to cover her nose. "Musty and damp, like a wet dog..."

"Or werewolf legs at the end of a run," quipped Resus. Suddenly, something cold and wet rubbed against his leg and he jumped, crying out.

"You know, for a scary vampire, you squeal a lot like a four-year-old." Luke grinned. "It's just Dig."

Resus crouched, his heart racing. "Dig!" he exclaimed, scratching the partial pooch under the chin. Then he leaned in and whispered in the dog's ear, "Please don't do that again! I don't know if I'll be able to find a spare pair of boxer shorts inside my cloak that easily!"

The vampire cloak Resus wore had been handed down through generations of the Negative family – always providing access to useful items kept in dozens of magical pockets hidden within the lining. However, since Resus had taken ownership, the cloak had become a little grouchy, possibly offended at being worn by a non-vampire. These days it frequently dispensed the wrong object, at precisely the wrong time – most likely just for fun.

Luke and Resus wandered further down the hallway. "Hello?" they called.

"I don't think anyone's in," said Cleo.

"We should still have a nose around, just to make sure," said Luke.

Cleo nodded. "Good idea!"

"Bad idea," whispered Resus as Luke knocked on, and then opened, the nearest door. "So obviously a bad idea!"

Luke and Cleo strode confidently into the next room. Resus held back for a few seconds, then, when he couldn't hear any sounds of pain or distress, peeked around the door.

There were pictures of houses on the walls in here, too. Resus peered at the one nearest the door. It was a hand-drawn sketch, mounted in an ornate frame of black ash. Others were old photographs, or watercolours.

Aside from the pictures, the room was completely empty.

"It could be an invisible family?" suggested Luke, waving his arms around in the air in an effort to touch something. "Poltergeists, maybe?"

"Well, I'd stop doing that, then," said Resus. "You might accidentally slap one of them in the face, and poltergeists aren't known for having the most restrained of tempers, remember?"

Luke thought back to the day he and his parents first arrived in Scream Street. Back then, the devious mayor, Sir Otto Sneer, had been making poltergeists of his own by hauling the spirits of the dead from their graves and zapping them with an electrical charge. He then used the surly spirits to cause chaos in the homes of anyone who dared to stand up against his wicked, money-making schemes.

Luke shuddered, quickly stuffing his hands into his pockets. "Yeah, maybe you're right."

"What if they're teeny tiny people?" gasped Cleo, lifting up her foot and studying the bandages underneath. "I hope we haven't stepped on anyone."

"Oh, don't say that!" whined Resus. "It's

yucky enough having to wipe Lulu's slime from the bottom of my shoes. A pet leech's goo is bad enough; I don't want to have to dispose of any squished little people as well!"

He carefully dropped to his knees and held his face a few centimetres away from the mouldy carpet. "Hello?" he whispered. "Are you all really, really small in here?"

"Why are you whispering?" asked Luke.

"Because if they are really tiny, then we probably look and sound like giants to them," Resus replied. "I don't want to hurt their ears."

"If they're really small, then either we've already stomped them into the carpet, or Dig's sniffed them up one of his nostrils," Cleo pointed out.

"Fair enough," said Resus, standing and brushing dirt from his knees.

"I can't imagine it's a tiny family," said Luke. "Why would someone build such a big house if the new residents were going to be microscopic?"

"I suppose they wouldn't," said Cleo. She watched Dig sniff around the edges of the room for a moment, then turned her attention to the pencil sketch on the wall. "Whoever does live here, they've really got a thing for houses," she said.

"Yeah, but not for furniture, or belongings ... or people," said Resus.

"I'll have a proper listen," said Luke with a wink.

Luke closed his eyes and concentrated. He used to have to try and control his temper in order to avoid triggering a dangerous werewolf transformation. But now that he was used to living in the magical atmosphere of Scream Street, he often found that he could safely change just one part of his body by focusing on how it would look in its hairy form, and channelling that energy in the right direction.

After a few seconds, Luke felt a familiar dark sensation wash over him. He pictured his ears growing larger and sliding up the sides of his face until they stood, tall and proud, on top of his head.

The change complete, Luke opened his eyes and listened carefully.

Everything sounded exactly the same — except that his two friends were now laughing.

"What's so funny?" he demanded.

"Not a lot." Resus chuckled. "Although we'll have quite a *tale* to tell when we get back home."

"Eh?" Luke reached up and touched his ears – which were still firmly stuck at the sides of his head and still distinctly human. So, which part of his body had transformed? He ran his hands down his arms and legs, but everything seemed to be the same.

"I don't get it," he said after a moment, his tail scraping against the wall as it flicked back and forth. "I was sure that I'd transformed someth—"

Resus and Cleo cracked up as Luke glanced behind him and caught sight of his wagging tail. Dig hurried over, wagging his own bony tail to join in with the fun.

"Very funny!" Luke grinned. "No idea why that went so wrong. I'll try again!"

This time, when Luke closed his eyes, he successfully managed to make his tail shrink and his ears grow into those of his werewolf.

"OK, quiet everyone," he said. He gestured for Resus, Cleo and Dig to remain silent, then he turned on the spot, listening as carefully as he could.

"Nope," he said eventually. "Still nothing."

"Nobody at home, then," said Cleo. "OK, let's go." She turned to find Resus already opening the door they had just come in through.

"Way ahead of you, Cleo!" he beamed.

The trio stepped back out into the hallway –
and froze. They weren't in the hallway at all.
This was a new room, with a boarded-over window in one wall and a set of metal lift doors at
the far end.

"That's weird," said Cleo.

"But that was definitely the door we came
through," said Resus, glancing behind them.
He jumped when he realized that the door had
completely vanished. "But ... but ... it was right
there!"

He hurried over to what was now a solid wall
and ran his fingers over the surface, hoping to
find a hidden door handle. There wasn't one.

"You see!" he cried, spinning to face his
friends. "*This* is why you don't walk into houses
belonging to people you don't know!"

"*Grrrr!*"

"It's no use getting angry at me, Luke!" he
continued. "I knew this was a bad idea from the
first second you mentioned it."

"What?" said Luke. "That wasn't me
growling!"

31

"No, it was Dig," said Cleo. "He's spotted something."

All three kids turned to look at the lift at the far end of the room. Above it, on the wall, was a semi-circular floor indicator with a large arrow. A large arrow that was slowly dropping from floor three, down to floor two, and below. The house began to vibrate as the lift's motor whirred closer and closer.

Resus started to breathe heavily. "I don't know who's in there, and I don't want to find out!" he exclaimed. With that, he turned to the boarded window and ran at it as fast as he could. At the last moment, he leapt into the air and slammed into the boards with his shoulder...

...only to bounce straight back off them.

"OK," he grunted. "Ow!"

"Stand aside," said Cleo, her eyes narrowing as she fixed the window as her target. With a piercing scream, she sprang into the air and hit the window with a flying kick. She crashed into the wood just like Resus had, and fell to the floor.

"OK," she said. "I agree. Ow!"

As Resus hurried over to help her up, Luke turned back to the lift. The arrow had almost reached their floor. The lift gave a loud *ding!*

"Guys," he said, as calmly as he could. "We've got company."

He raised his hands and clenched his fists. Cleo took her place beside him and struck a threatening martial-arts stance. Dig crouched and growled deep in his throat.

Resus hid behind them all, peeking through his trembling fingers.

Then the lift doors began to open.

Chapter Three
THE LIFT

As the lift doors squeaked open, Resus let out an involuntary squeal, making Luke and Cleo jump.

"Again with the four-year-old's scream!" Luke exclaimed.

"*You're* the only thing scaring us!" cried Cleo.

But Resus wasn't listening. Instead he stood trembling, his false fangs chattering as his bottom lip wobbled.

"I'm so sorry!" he blubbed.

"Resus..." said Luke.

But Resus ignored his friend. He took a step forward, eyes squeezed tightly shut. He slowly shuffled towards the end of the room and the open lift. "We shouldn't have come in here, we know that!"

"Resus!" said Cleo.

Resus raised his hands and waved them apologetically. "We won't do it again! We promise!"

"*Resus!*" yelled Luke and Cleo together.

Resus opened his eyes with a start. "What?" he shouted. "Can't you see I'm busy pleading for our— Oh, the lift's empty!"

It was true; there was nothing inside the lift at all. It was just a vacant metal box.

The vampire turned to his pals, trying hard not to blush beneath his pale face paint. "Of course, I knew that was a possibility all along," he said.

Luke scowled at him.

"What?" Resus demanded. "I was right with you, all along."

"Oh, really?" said Cleo, folding her arms.

"Of course!" said Resus, karate-chopping at the air. "Just then, I was lulling them into a false sense of security."

Luke shook his head and stepped into the lift.

"Yeah, right."

"Whoa!" yelled Resus. "What in the name of all things sharp and pointy do you think you're doing?"

"There's no other way out," said Luke with a shrug.

Resus shook his head. "I don't know what the Scream Street record for the most bad ideas in one day is, but you must be getting pretty close!"

Cleo and Dig joined Luke inside the lift. Resus stubbornly remained standing on the spot outside.

"Come on!" Luke urged.

"No chance!" Resus insisted.

The lift doors began to close again.

"Did you press a button?" asked Cleo, scanning the bare metal walls for anything that might keep the doors open.

"I can't even *see* any buttons!" Luke replied. "Come on, Resus," he said, gesturing for the vampire to join them. "This could be your only chance!"

"What? My only chance to be needlessly slaughtered by whatever is waiting for us at the end of that lift ride, you mean?" asked Resus. "Nope, I'm staying right—"

Splat!

A large lump of sticky green slime dropped from above and landed squarely on Resus's head.

"Bleurrgh!" cried Resus, reaching up to touch the stuff. The goo was warm, wet and smelled like the inside of a zombie's sleeping bag. The vampire looked up to see a vast puddle of the stuff pooling out across the ceiling — and another large dollop slowly stringing down towards his face.

"Argh!" With a mighty jump, Resus leapt for the closing lift doors, making it through just as they slammed together ominously.

"That stuff touched me!" he cried, flapping his hands wildly to get the gunk off his fingers. "It touched me!"

He plunged a hand inside his cloak and pulled out the first piece of material he could find: a pair of gleaming white boxer shorts. "Oh great," he hissed to his cloak. "Bet you wouldn't have given me these earlier if I'd needed them, would you?"

With no other cloth available, Resus wadded up the pants and used them to clean the green goo from his hair.

"This is the worst day ever," he moaned. He looked up to find Luke and Cleo smiling at him.

"What are you two so happy about?"

"Admit it," said Luke. "You want to know what monster lives in this house just as much as we do." He rubbed his hands together eagerly. "I hope it's something new and exciting!"

"That collects old pictures of houses?" said Cleo. "Doesn't seem very likely."

"I just hope it's vegetarian," said Resus, tucking the slime-covered boxer shorts back inside his cloak.

The trio stood in silence for a moment, watching as the arrow above the doorway cranked down to the letter "B".

Eventually there was a *thud* as the carriage reached the bottom of the lift shaft. The lights above the kids flickered, and the bell gave out another *ding!* With the screech of metal scraping on metal, the doors began to slowly open.

Back at the Watsons' house, Mike sat at the dinner table, toying with a cold stem of broccoli. He carefully balanced the vegetable on his plate, then flicked it across the room with his finger.

"I was really looking forward to that!" he groaned.

"What?" asked Sue, retrieving the broken bit of broccoli and dumping it into the bowl of cold vegetables she was taking to the bin in the kitchen. "The broccoli? You probably shouldn't be firing it at the wallpaper, then."

Mike sniffed. "Not just the broccoli," he said. "The potatoes too. And the carrots. And, most of all, the roast chicken."

"Well, you never know," said Sue as she left the room, "it might come back."

"Are you saying it's a homing chicken?" asked Mike. "You think it might come home to *roast*?" Despite his gloom, he allowed himself a small smile at the pun — but quickly hid it when Sue reappeared.

"I just wanted a normal Sunday at home!" he moaned.

"No, you didn't," said Sue, collecting the cutlery. "You wanted one of our *old* Sundays, back before we knew Luke was a werewolf. You don't know what a 'normal' Sunday is like here in Scream Street. You're always skulking at home, moping about something."

Mike sat upright, and thought for a second. "You know, you're right!" he said. "Sundays might be fantastic here in Scream Street. I'll never know until I try. You should have mentioned this before."

"What?" cried Sue, her eyes wide. "I'm always telling you to—"

"From this moment on," announced Mike, interrupting her, "I shall immerse myself in my new home – Scream Street. We both will! And we'll start by following Luke's lead and going to welcome our new neighbours."

"If you say so, dear," said Sue, trying to hide her smile. "If we hurry, we should be able to catch—"

"Oh, I can't go right this minute," said Mike, as he jumped to his feet and headed for the kitchen. "I've got an idea!"

Sue sighed and sat down at the table again. "Of course you have."

The lift doors opened, and the trio found themselves staring into a large underground room. The walls were painted a sickly green colour, and there were purple and red pipes running in every direction. Clear ooze ran down every surface, and steam billowed from unseen vents.

The worst part was the pile of chalk-white

bones and skulls that littered the floor. Bones and skulls that looked very human.

Luke was the first to step out of the lift. He bent to pick up what was possibly a rib. "Well," he said as cheerfully as he could. "We're not the first to come down here." He casually tossed the rib over his shoulder onto the floor. Dig was on it in a flash, chomping and biting at the unexpected treat.

Cleo crossed the room — taking great care not to trip on a length of spine that lay in her path — and ran a bandaged hand over one of the walls. Her palm came away dripping with clear goo. "These walls are really ... slimy!" she said, holding up her hand.

Resus, on the other side of the room, had made a similar discovery. "Weird," he said, pressing his own hand against the wall. "It's all squidgy and warm." Whatever the wall was made of, it gave a little under his touch, like lukewarm rubber.

Meanwhile, Luke had turned his attention to a collection of pipes running from floor to ceiling in the centre of the room. One of them in particular — a purple pipe about as thick as his arm — caught his eye, and he wrapped his hands around it.

The pipe pumped, no, *throbbed* under his touch. Luke swallowed hard. "Er, guys," he said. "Feel this pipe."

Resus and Cleo clambered over the scattered bones to join him and clutch the pipe with their own hands. They shared a worried glance.

"Is it just me," Luke continued, "or does that feel a lot like a pulse?"

Resus screwed his eyes shut. "Oh no," he groaned. "No, no, no. Please don't say it..."

Suddenly, Cleo gasped as the truth hit her. "The house is alive!"

"There it is," sighed Resus. "She said it!"

Chapter Four
THE ACID

Resus stared hard into his friends' eyes. "There are no monsters in this house because this house *is* the monster!"

"The pictures..." added Cleo. "They're family portraits!"

"We walked right into its mouth!" cried Luke. "We need to get out of here, now!"

The kids turned back to the lift, but the doors were tightly closed, and the arrow above was rising up to floor three. Resus searched the dripping wall on either side of the lift for a button to call the carriage back down, but there was nothing.

"This way!" yelled Luke, racing for a door at the other end of the room. Skipping and jumping over the bones, Cleo and Resus followed him through it — only to appear back in the same room through a door in the opposite wall.

"What?" asked Resus. "But, how...?"

"Never mind!" Cleo shouted. "Keep running!"

The vampire didn't need telling twice, turning and darting for a different door. He gripped the handle, flung it open and ran through. Once again, he arrived back in the same room, just in another part of it.

Luke and Cleo were having the same problem. Whichever door they chose as an exit turned out to be an entrance back into the bone-strewn expanse. Dig trotted after them, pausing every now and again to sniff at a tasty-looking leg bone or pelvis.

After a few tries, Resus gave up and sat on a nearby pile of bones. He watched his friends race back and forth for a moment, then chose a couple of skulls from the collection at his feet.

44

Sliding his fingers into the backs, he held them up and operated them like a pair of puppets.

"Now I look back at it, Cleo, I wish I'd listened to Resus!" said one skull.

"Yes, Luke," said the other. "Then we wouldn't have ended up dead!"

A sturdy arm bone bounced off his head with a *bonk!* He looked up to see Cleo glaring down at him, arms folded.

"... is the first gargoyle to suffer from a fear of heights," announced Anna Gored, the zombie newsreader on the Magic Mirror, Scream Street's version of a TV.

"Now, reports just in that a criminal monster has escaped from its imprisonment in the Underlands," she continued. "It is highly dangerous. Members of the public are advised not to—"

Click!

Mike grabbed the wand that acted as a remote control and switched channels to the ghostly motoring show, *Top Fear*. Then he went back to mixing ingredients in a large bowl.

Sue entered the kitchen and stopped at the

sight of her husband in his flower-patterned apron. "A cake?" She chuckled. "You're baking a cake?"

"Of course!" said Mike, beaming and adding a little extra butter to his mixture. "What better way to welcome our new neighbours?"

"If you say so," said Sue, smiling. She selected a mug from the cupboard and poured herself a cup of coffee. She had a long wait ahead of her.

"Has Luke gone over already?" asked Mike.

Sue nodded. "Yes. He's gone ahead with his pals."

Mike sighed happily. "Well, say what you like about Scream Street, but at least Luke's made some proper friends here. It's nice to see them getting on so well."

"Oh, I knew your stupid curiosity would get us killed!" Resus bellowed. "Just because a door is open, it doesn't mean you have to go in!"

"You didn't *have* to come along!" Luke shouted back.

The boys were nose to nose in the middle of the room, jabbing each other in the chest as they argued.

were now stained and smeared with the same green gunk that had fallen on Resus upstairs.

"Eurgh, that stuff!" the vampire cried. "Don't get any of it on me! It reeks!"

Scowling, Cleo scooped a handful of the goo from her head and threw it at him. "Today can't get much worse!" she sighed.

Then the trapdoor in the ceiling slammed shut, the bandage was severed and Cleo crashed to the ground. An alarm sounded, and something liquid and nasty began to flow into the room from a series of taps set into the walls.

"It just got worse, didn't it?" groaned the mummy.

Luke grabbed Cleo's hand and pulled her to her feet. "It's some kind of acid!" he said, peering at the hissing fluid.

"Acid?" exclaimed Cleo.

The three began to back away from the encroaching green-brown river.

"I guess a living house has to have a stomach," Luke mused. "And stomachs use acid to digest..." His voice trailed away.

"Oh, fantastic!" cried Resus. "Now we're dinner! Perfect!"

Mike stuck his tongue out of the corner of his mouth as he carefully iced a message on the top of his completed cake.

"Welcome to Scream Street," he read aloud. "And they are totally *welcome* to it!" He looked up as Sue entered. "Any sign of Luke?"

"Nope!"

Mike paused his piping and sat back in his seat, gazing off into an unseen distance. "What I wouldn't give to be Luke's age again. Mucking around with my mates. Not a care in the world!"

"It's all my fault!" Luke wailed to his friends. "But I got you both into this, and I'll get you out!"

The kids were standing on a small raised plinth in the centre of the room. The floor had almost completely vanished beneath a bubbling pool of stomach acid.

Luke closed his eyes and pictured his were-wolf's powerful hands. Within seconds, he felt the familiar dark shadow sweeping down from his shoulders as his lower arms transformed. Long, yellow talons burst from the ends of his fingers

and his palms swelled up. Thick, dense fur erupted from every pore.

The arm transformation complete, Luke leapt over the advancing sea of acid, digging his claws into the walls and gouging grooves into the warm surface as he landed. Then he began to punch and pummel the wall as hard as he could.

Luke roared in fury as he fought to create an escape route. But it was no good. Even his strong wolf paws weren't making much more than a small dent.

There was a *hisssss*, and Luke looked down to find the stomach acid pooling around his feet. Plumes of stinking steam rose up from his trainers as they began to dissolve.

Jumping back onto the plinth, Luke allowed his hands to return to normal. "It's no good," he moaned. "I didn't do anything!"

"Yes, you did!" said Cleo, pointing to the arrow on the wall above the lift. "When you smashed the walls, the lift started to come down again."

Luke peered towards the lift through eyes that were beginning to sting and weep. The arrow had paused below floor two, but was now beginning

to creep back up to three.

"We need to cause this house as much stomach pain as possible – and quickly!" said Resus, as the ocean of bile continued to rise around them. "Luke, you need to step into the acid again."

"But..."

"You can get us out of this!" Resus urged. "But not as you. We need the wolf!"

"No," said Luke, shaking his head. "I can't control it. You won't be safe."

"We're not safe anyway," Resus pointed out. "It's our only chance!"

Luke stood firm. "No way!" he snarled.

"Then I'm really sorry mate," said Resus earnestly, and he pushed his best friend off the plinth and straight into the burning acid.

Chapter Five
THE WOLF

Luke's feet splashed into the bubbling lake of stomach acid that surrounded the central plinth. The meagre layers of protection that were his trainers and socks quickly dissolved, and the fierce liquid began to bite into his skin. He was being digested!

A bolt of pain shot up Luke's legs, causing him to cry out in agony. His vision blurred and his hearing grew muffled as the oncoming werewolf transformation engulfed him completely.

Bones cracked as his face reshaped, a long vulpine snout stretching out as sharp teeth burst from his gums. His spine cracked and reformed: longer, curvier and thicker. Yellow talons skewered their way out of his fingertips, tearing his own nails away as his knuckles twisted into new, more animalistic shapes.

Then came the coating of fur — coarse brown hair that forced its way through his skin. His tail grew, his ears rose up, and his ribs adjusted as his internal organs completed their unseen change.

Resus and Cleo shared a nervous glance. Their friend was gone and in his place stood a ferocious werewolf. Whatever the creature did next, it would be the end of their adventure. What they didn't know was how many of them would walk away from it alive.

"Ready, Cleo?" Resus asked, reaching out to squeeze his friend's hand.

Cleo cricked her neck from side to side. "Been ready for centuries!" She grinned.

"Then run!"

Resus leapt off the plinth and ran through the lake of acid as quickly as he could. The wolf's yellow eyes twitched to follow him, then the

creature focused back on Cleo. She scanned the room and raced off in the opposite direction.

The werewolf gave chase, its furry feet splashing through the stomach bile as easily as paddling in the ocean at the seaside.

Cleo reached the far wall and jumped high, planting her feet on the warm surface, then flipped herself up and over.

Spinning effortlessly in the air, she landed behind the monster. The wolf couldn't stop itself in time and crashed hard into the wall.

Above the lift, the arrow began to drop down from the third floor.

Stunned, the wolf turned to find Resus in its field of vision. Ignoring the plumes of acidic steam rising from his shoes, Resus lifted up his cloak matador-style and called out in the best Spanish accent he could muster, "Olé! Wolfy boy! Resus is ready for you!"

The wolf snorted angrily and ran for its prey. Resus held his nerve and stayed on the spot, waving his cloak until the very last moment. Then he jumped to the side, allowing the werewolf to thunder past and collide with the wall behind.

Grrrrooooooaaaaannnn!

The noise came from all around them, as though the house was crying out in pain.

"It's working!" cried Resus. "Keep going!"

"Oi! Smelly legs!" yelled Cleo, struggling to stay on her feet as the wall behind her began to heave in and out. The wolf raced towards her, only for Cleo to launch herself up into the air, feet spread wide as she executed a perfect split. The werewolf tried to stop, but slipped in the acid and fell, burning its tail and bottom in the gunge as it collided with the wall.

As the wolf howled again – this time more in pain than in anger – the arrow above the lift dipped below the second floor, and kept falling.

The werewolf jumped to its feet, the veins in the side of its head throbbing as wave after wave of rage washed over it. This was the version of the wolf that Resus and Cleo had always feared. Luke was trapped deep inside, with no way to control it and no way to escape.

But this was the version of the wolf they were banking on to save their lives.

"Over here, furry pants!" cried Resus, his back pressed against one of the doors they had tried to leave the room through earlier. On either side of the exit, the walls pulsed in and out angrily, sending wave after wave of acid sploshing around the room. There was not much left of Resus's patent leather shoes now, and the vampire couldn't begin to imagine what sort of pain Cleo was in with just her bandages to protect her. But burned feet were the least of his worries — the wolf was running directly at him again.

Resus turned and pulled at the handle — but the door wouldn't move! He tried again, twisting and tugging, but it was no good. He could hear the splashes and snarls as his best friend's anarchic alter ego came closer and closer.

The vampire began to panic. Had the house locked them in here? No — it was the walls! They were writhing around in so much pain that they were wedging the door closed. Resus could almost feel the werewolf's hot breath on the back of his neck, and there was no way out.

Unless...

Resus knew he didn't have time to turn, so he listened hard for the wolf's attack and at the last moment dived head-first into the sea of acid.

He felt the burning gloop begin to eat at his

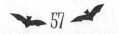

skin and knew he wouldn't be able to stay under for very long.

Crash!

Resus heard — and felt — the wolf hit the door above him, and he took the chance to push himself away from the wall with his feet. When he couldn't take the acid's sting any longer, he forced his head up and out of the liquid, taking in great gulps of the stale yet delicious air.

Cleo pulled him out of the acid and quickly began to wipe the goo off what remained of his clothing with clumps of her bandages. Amazingly, his vampire cloak was untouched. "I think that's what saved you from really getting hurt!" she said.

"Thanks!" Resus whispered into his cloak.

Now it was Dig's turn to tease their attacker. Hopping on his two skeletal back legs like some sort of wannabe wallaby, he darted past the wolf. The creature swung out with its huge paw, missing Dig's ear by a centimetre but causing the wolf to overbalance again. It fell against the nearest collection of pipes, which were now pulsing in and out as much as the walls around them.

Grrrrrroooooooooaaaaaaaannnnnn!

The house bellowed again, forcing Resus to press his hands against his ears for a second. He glanced over at the lift. The arrow showed it had passed below the ground floor and was descending quickly to the basement.

"One more push should do it!" he cried.

The wolf shook its head to clear its vision, then its ears twitched. Over the squishy wet noise of the walls contracting and expanding, and the groaning of the building around them, it could hear a canine growl.

Its piercing yellow eyes focused on a squat figure on the opposite side of the room. It was Dig again, his hackles raised and teeth bared. He was challenging the wolf for the position of pack leader.

Furious, the wolf ran towards its prey. There would be no mistake this time, no more slips or trips. No twists or turns. The creature was going to grab that insubordinate dog between its jaws, and—

Suddenly, a long length of bandage rose up from the stomach acid and pulled tight. The wolf just had time to glance either side to see Resus and Cleo pulling hard on the ends of the material before its legs were swept from beneath it. The monster's momentum kept it moving, and it slammed into the wall, face first.

Grrrrrrrrrooooooooooooaaaaaaaaannnnnnn!

Ding!

The lift's doors screeched open. Resus, Cleo and Dig raced for the gloomy car and jumped inside — quickly followed by the werewolf. It turned and snarled at them as the doors closed.

"Perfect!" said Resus. "Trapped in a tin box with a ravenous beastie!"

The lift began to rise steadily, and Cleo took a step forward. "Luke!" she yelled. "We know you're in there somewhere!"

"Er, Cleo..." said Resus.

"Not now!" Cleo snapped. "Luke, you have to hear us."

"Cleo!"

The mummy ignored him.

"This is our only means of escape, Luke," she said sternly. "So you have to take control of the wolf, and—"

"*Cleo!*"

Cleo spun to face Resus. "What is it?"

Resus pointed at the arrow on the display

above the door. "Look how fast we're going!"

Cleo, Dig and the wolf all followed Resus's gaze. The arrow was spinning around and around, like the blade of a fan. They could feel the carriage rocking from side to side as they continued to accelerate.

Luke's werewolf gave a tiny *yelp*.

Just at that moment, Luke's parents arrived at the front door of the new house, bearing the finished cake.

"Are you OK?" Sue asked her husband.

"Of course!" replied Mike, trying to stop his knees from knocking together. "But, just to say, if anything weird happens—"

Boom!

An explosion rocked the woods as something burst out from the roof of the house. The Watsons looked up to see what appeared to be a metal wardrobe rocketing up into the sky.

"Oh, good grief!" groaned Mike.

After a few seconds, the lift reached its peak altitude, then it began to fall — right towards where the Watsons were standing. Sue grabbed Mike's shirt and pulled him away just in time.

The lift slammed into the ground, then bounced up again, its doors buckling. Resus, Cleo and Dig were jolted out, all three of them landing together, shaken and disoriented.

Mike had taken a cautious step forward, the cake still clutched in his hands, when the twisted metal box landed back down with a *thud*. With a furious growl, the werewolf leapt out and faced him.

"Aarrgh!" squealed Mike, tossing the cake into the air.

Resus rubbed at a bruise on his knee. "And you lot reckon *I* scream like a four-year-old."

The werewolf took a step forward, before the cake landed on its head with a *splat!* The shock was enough to send the creature crashing backwards. By the time it had hit the ground, the wolf had reverted to Luke again.

Mike trembled, looking around. "Well, I think that's probably enough surprises for one day!" he said.

"Look!" cried Cleo, pointing to the monster house as it vanished into thin air.

This was finally too much for Mike. He swooned, falling into his wife's arms.

"So," said Luke, "anybody want some cake?"

His mum and Cleo laughed, then Resus joined in as the one-legged roast chicken hopped past them. Dig's skeletal tail began to wag hard and, with the happiest of *yips*, he gave chase.

WOLF GANG

Chapter One
THE FLYER

Dig the dog sat in Scream Street's central square, scratching his ear with one of his back paws. Suddenly, the animal froze and sniffed at the air. He could smell something pleasant. Something succulent. Something crunchy he'd like to sink his teeth into.

Breakfast!

He could smell a juicy bone, and ... *sniff, sniff* ... it was somewhere just behind him.

Yowf!

Jumping up, Dig spun around, expecting to find a tasty treat waiting there for him to devour. But there was nothing there. That was strange... He sniffed at the air again and found he could still smell the bone. It was behind him again. His breakfast was moving!

Ruff!

Dig flipped over to face back the other way. Nothing! This was proving quite a challenge. No matter which way he faced, the delicious aroma of fresh bone was always behind him.

He paused to scratch another itch – this time on his nose – and raised his back paw again to tackle the tickle. Suddenly, there it was! A flash of white and a powerful waft of tasty marrow. It was the bone!

Crunch!

Dig sank his teeth into the bone, and then—

Howl!

He let it go just as quickly. He sighed – in as much as a dog could sigh. He'd done it again. He'd completely forgotten that, from the middle backwards, he was nothing but skeleton. He'd been smelling his own back leg, and had just tried to eat it. What a half-witted hound! Still, it wasn't as bad as the time he'd tried to bury his bottom in Dr Skully's back garden.

Dig glanced around Scream Street to make sure no one had seen his cannibalistic clanger. Thankfully, the place was as deserted as it usually was at this hour of the morning. The night ghouls had all retired to their coffins, and it was still too early for the creatures that roamed during the day to be up and about.

There was still a big question on his mind, though. Where was he going to find breakfast?

Dig sniffed at the air again, and picked up a new scent. This one was different. It had travelled a distance to reach his searching snout. This was the smell of fear and that usually meant an animal in distress. In other words: easy prey.

Nostrils quivering, Dig trotted across the square to one of the roads on the far side. The smell was stronger now. Whatever was giving off the aroma was definitely scared. Dig's trot became a proud stride. Perhaps this poor creature had heard about Dig's incredible hunting skills, and was at this very moment lying in fear of being discovered by the menacing mutt?

Creak!

Dig's ears twitched. That was the sound of a door opening slightly. Now the smell of fear was almost overpowering – to the point where he could actually see it. It hung in the air like a trail of yellow mist. And it was leading directly to the haunted-looking house at number 13, Scream Street.

Squeezing through a broken board in the fence, Dig raced up to the partially open front door and finally located the source of the stench. It was a human male. A human male that was crouching on all fours behind the door and peering nervously outside.

Dig was pretty certain that this wasn't breakfast after all, but he gave the human's face a good lick, just to make sure.

"Yuck!" cried Mike Watson, wiping the doggy drool from his cheek. "Go away, boy! Shoo! Now!"

Exasperated, and sighing another dog sigh, Dig turned and trotted away in search of another source of food. He was almost certain he'd smelt a nice juicy bone behind him.

Left alone, Mike climbed to his feet, but didn't open the door any further. His eyes scanned the garden, then fell on the rusting metal mailbox with the name "Watson" daubed on the side in dripping red paint. The flag was up – which meant there were letters inside. It also meant he had to go all the way down to the garden gate to fetch them.

Finally swinging the door open, Mike took a tentative step outside. He paused for a second – waiting for some monster to pounce on him – but nothing happened.

Everything seemed quiet and calm, and that worried him. By now, there was usually a zombie's hand pushing its way up through the flowerbed, or a colony of bats whizzing around his head and pulling at his hair. Today, however, he was completely alone.

Mike allowed himself a deep breath. This was more like it. No crazy creatures to set his heart pounding, or nightmare neighbours to make him jump out of his skin. He was just a normal guy, collecting his post.

He strode down to the mailbox and flipped it open casually. Inside was a collection of letters and flyers – a usual day's delivery. Nothing to be worried about at all.

He had just retrieved the letters from the box and was beginning to flick through them when the air shivered. Something tall and black blurred into view and, with a screech of leather shoes, a vampire stood within striking distance.

"Morning!" cried Alston Negative from his side of the fence.

By the time Mike opened his mouth to scream, his body had already left the ground. The terrified leap he performed wouldn't have won any awards for style, but his perfect landing on top of the garden gate was nothing if not impressive.

"Did I make you jump?" asked Alston, as he collected his own post.

The gate squeaked as Mike swung slowly from side to side. "Er..."

"Sorry about that," said Alston. "Did you sleep well?"

"I haven't since arriving in Scream Street, no," Mike admitted as he clambered down from the gate to pick up his scattered post from the lawn.

"You should try a nice, comfy, velvet-lined coffin!" suggested Alston.

Mike's fake grin lasted until he could get back inside the house and slam the door. "A coffin is

precisely what I'm trying to avoid!" he sighed, slumping back against the door.

He was indoors again, safe from shocks, jumps and frights. The beautiful melody of the classical music he'd put on earlier came tripping through the air, and he managed to calm his breathing before joining his wife, Sue, in the kitchen. She handed him a cup of tea.

"Anything interesting?" she asked, gesturing to the pile of post.

"Nope," he said, sipping his drink. "Not unless you're a fan of bills or junk mail."

Ah, here it came! His favourite bit of the symphony. Mike closed his eyes and imagined he was standing before an orchestra, a baton in his hand.

He sighed happily and began to conduct the musicians in his mind. The mellow drag of the string section; the playful tootling of the woodwind players; the horrible, nasty sound of someone operating on an angry cat...

Mike's eyes shot wide open. "Gaaah! What on earth is that awful racket?" he demanded.

Sue glanced up at the ceiling. She winced. "That's Luke, practising upstairs for his exam."

"He's got an exam in torturing people's

eardrums?"

"Believe it or not, that's supposed to be music," said Sue. "And don't blame me – you're the one who bought that old piano from the classified ads in *The Terror Times*."

"I did," said Mike. "But not so that Luke could attack it with a sledgehammer!" He grabbed the broom and began to knock on the ceiling with the handle. "Do you mind?"

The cacophony stopped as quickly as it had started. Then, following a door slam upstairs, Luke appeared, sliding down the banister. He dropped lightly to the floor, in front of his father.

"Hey, Dad," said Luke. "Do you want me to pass my music exam, or don't you?"

Mike nodded. "Yes, but you've got months to go before—"

"It's on Wednesday," Luke interrupted.

"Wednesday?" exclaimed Mike. "Well, maybe they'll *like* your horrific playing. This *is* Scream Street, after all."

"Dad!"

"Seriously, Luke, how on earth are we going to turn you into a musical prodigy in just three days?"

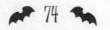

74

"We could hire a home tutor," suggested Luke's mum, appearing in the doorway to the kitchen. She held up a flyer she'd found among the junk mail.

"Great idea!" said Mike.

Luke, however, was horrified. "Really? I go to school, then I come home and go to school again? No thank you!"

Mike took the flyer from his wife and read it aloud. "Music tuition, call Wolfgang." He paused to turn the piece of paper over, but the reverse side was blank. "That's odd, there's no number. How are we supposed to call him?"

Sue shrugged. "Maybe like this?" She cupped her hands around her mouth and called out, "Wolfgang?"

A ghostly head with flowing white hair appeared through the wall. "You called?" it grinned.

This time, Mike landed on the banister.

Chapter Two
THE TUTOR

"A ghost!" said Luke. "Cool!" Extra lessons didn't seem so bad if they involved a spirit from beyond the grave.

"No!" came Mike's strangled yelp from his perch. "That was *not* cool!"

The Watsons watched as the ghost stepped completely out of the wall. He was a tall man, dressed in a long red tailcoat, matching scarlet trousers and smart black boots.

The spooky figure bowed deeply. "Wolfgang

van Mozhoven, at your service!" he announced in a thick German accent.

Mike climbed down from the banister. "No, no, no!" he cried. "A ghost tutoring my son? Over my dead body!"

Wolfgang began to chuckle. "Ghost? Dead body? You make ze joke? Ha, ha, ha, ha. Ve are going to make very funny time together!"

"Darling," said Sue to her husband, kindly. "It's not like we've got many other options."

"Ya," said Wolfgang. "I am ze greatest composer ever — even if mein body is doing ze exact opposite — decomposing." The ghost giggled hysterically. "Anozer little joke for you funny fans out zare!"

Mike's eyes narrowed, and he scanned the names on his collection of classical records. "How come I've never heard of you?"

Wolfgang sighed long and hard. "Sadly, I was dead before I could be writing mein brilliant second symphony. Sob, sob, sad violins."

"Oh, come on, Dad!" Luke urged. "I need all the help I can get, and you know you don't want Dr Skully to call you in to school for a chat about my work."

Mike pictured himself standing in a queue to talk to Luke's skeletal teacher behind the assortment of gruesome ghouls and mumbling monsters that made up Scream Street's residents. He quickly shook his head to clear the terrible vision.

"OK," he sighed.

"Yahoo!" cried Wolfgang, clapping his hands in glee. "You von't regret this!"

Mike shuddered. "I am a bit, already," he said.

Brrrriiiinnnngggggggg!

Luke and his best friend, Resus Negative, arrived at Dr Skully's house just as the bell was ringing for the start of school.

Dr Skully, their teacher, had spent 50 years as an educational model skeleton, standing silently in the corner of a university lecture theatre, soaking up information from thousands of classes on every possible subject. Now retired from modeling, Dr Skully had converted his home into a school in order to pass that information on to the young residents of Scream Street.

Luke glanced in through the window as he and Resus approached the door. Luella Everwell – a young witch – was standing at the blackboard, writing out lines. Or, rather, she was just watching as three pieces of animated chalk flew across the board, doing the work for her. Slowly, the words "I must not use spells at school" were appearing dozens and dozens of times.

"Dr Skully won't be happy if he catches Luella doing that," said Luke.

"Too right," said Resus. "He's got a real thing against using magic in class. I still haven't got my enchanted pencil sharpener back since he confiscated it."

Luke looked at his friend. "Enchanted pencil sharpener?"

"Hey, it's hard work turning pencils!" cried Resus.

"You are the laziest vampire I know," scoffed Luke.

Resus shrugged. "Not bad, considering you only know three."

The boys heard footsteps and turned to find Cleo Farr racing to catch up. The Egyptian mummy looked flushed beneath her bandages.

"Guys, I've been searching everywhere for you!" she said.

"Why?" asked Luke. "Is there a problem?"

Cleo nodded. "Yes, and I need your help!"

"'Course we'll help," said Resus, dropping his backpack. "What's wrong?"

"OK," said Cleo. "We have the music exam in a few days, right?"

Luke nodded. "And?"

"And I'm so good at so many instruments, I can't decide which one to play!"

She looked up to find the boys scowling at her. "What?"

"It's a shame the embalmer didn't bandage your mouth up too," said Resus, stooping to pick up his bag.

"You had us going there for a second," Luke muttered.

"So, will you help, or what?" demanded Cleo. The boys didn't reply.

"Oh, like it's my fault I've had centuries to master all the instruments!"

"Well, I won't need centuries," said Luke with a smile. "I'll have you know that my parents have just hired me a personal piano tutor."

"Yep," said Resus flatly. "You're the lucky one, all right."

Cleo folded her arms.

"What now?" asked Luke.

"You've only got two days before the exam," said Cleo. "There's no way you're going to get as good as..."

Luke raised an eyebrow. "As good as what?"

"Well, as good as me!" Cleo finished.

Luke, never one to turn down a challenge, stuck out his hand. "We'll see about that!" he said, as Cleo shook it.

That evening, Mike sat in his favourite armchair, wearing the largest pair of headphones he'd been able to buy at Eefa's Emporium that afternoon. Each ear was covered by an enormous yellow hemisphere, making him look like a giant bug. The cable at the other end was plugged into Mike's precious stereo system.

He was lost in a world of conducting again. Grabbing the teaspoon from his cuppa, he waved it in the air, bringing the horn section into play. Then he turned to the harpist, gently indicating that she should pluck at her delicate strings and paint the piece with an air of mystery.

 81

His wife entered the room and stood watching for a moment, hands on hips.

"Are you going to sit there like that all night?"

Mike opened his eyes. He thought he'd heard someone talking over the music, but he couldn't be sure. He spotted Sue and smiled.

"Oh, hello dear!" he said loudly.

Sue sighed. "I said, are you going to sit there like that all night?"

"What?" cried Mike, not taking off his headphones. "Who's having a fight?"

"Not *fight!*" exclaimed Sue. "All *night!*"

"Oh," said Mike, giving her a thumbs-up. "Yes, that would be great, thanks. With mashed potatoes, if you don't mind."

Sue reached over and lifted the needle from the record. "I'm not wasting the next hour trying to have this conversation," she said.

Mike pulled off his headphones. "What's wrong?" he asked. "I thought we were talking about—"

Suddenly, a horrible clanking noise rang out from upstairs. It sounded as though someone had taken the bells from the Scream Street clock tower and was tossing them down the stairs.

 82

"Aaargh!" yelled Mike, jumping to his feet. "Poltergeists!"

"Calm down," said Sue. "It's only Luke, practising for his exam."

"But isn't Wolfgang with him? I would have thought that Luke would be getting better by now."

Sue nodded. "That's just what I was thinking."

"Ya... Ya... Nein! Nein! Nein!" Wolfgang paced up and down in the bedroom as Luke continued to batter at the piano keys like he was playing a rousing game of Whack-a-Goblin.

"Gently... Tempo! Allegro!"

Luke's fingers raced up and down the keys, hammering combinations at random in the hope that some of them might match the dots on the sheet of music he was pretending to read.

"*Stop!*" screeched Wolfgang eventually. "Zis tune will soon be a ghost like me because you are killing it, ya? Ha, ha, ha. But seriously, you are terrible."

Luke stood up. "Well then, Mr Musical Genius, why don't you show me how it's done?"

Wolfgang sat on the piano stool and stared

 83

longingly down at the keys. "I vould love to, but zare is a slight problem with zat..." He paused to crack his knuckles noisily, then spread his fingers and lay them down onto the keys. His hands went right through the wood of the piano.

"Of course!" gasped Luke. "You're a ghost! You can't play any more."

"Zat is so true!" moaned Wolfgang. "Sob, sob, sad violins." He turned to smile wickedly at Luke. "Alzough zare is one way I could be showing you how to play. I vould just need to be borrowing somezing first."

"Sure!" said Luke. "Name it, and it's yours!"

Suddenly, the lights in the room flickered and dimmed. Wolfgang stood and turned to glower down at Luke. He reached out with his ghostly, shimmering hand. Luke instinctively backed away, but quickly found himself trapped against the door.

Wolfgang continued his eerie advance. Luke could only watch as the composer's hand slid through his T-shirt and into his chest. He felt his heart grow cold as though it were gripped in an icy fist. Then, without warning, the ghost jumped forward, completely disappearing inside him.

Luke opened his mouth to speak, but what emerged was Wolfgang's German accent.

"I need to borrow your body!" he cackled. "Ha, ha, ha, ha!"

Chapter Three
THE DEAL

Luke's fingers flew across the piano keys like butterflies dancing in a shaft of summer light. The music he was playing was exquisite.

Downstairs, in the kitchen, his parents were frozen in the middle of cooking dinner. The milk Mike was pouring into the saucepan on the stove was beginning to overflow. It hit the gas flame with a *hiss* and ran down the side of the cooker.

"Can... Can you hear that?" he asked eventually.

Sue nodded slowly. "It's music."

"Proper music," Mike added. "With all the right notes, in the right order!"

"You don't think..." began Sue.

"No," said her husband. "It couldn't be! Could it?"

Turning off the stove and leaving dinner uncooked, the Watsons crept up the stairs, eager to find out just who was playing the incredible music. They paused outside Luke's bedroom door.

"Go on," urged Sue.

Mike adjusted the headphones, which were now hanging around his neck. "OK," he gulped.

Gripping the handle, he swung open the door, almost unable to look. He squinted into the room, and... Yes! It *was* Luke playing the piano! Mike stood and watched his son for a moment.

"Oh, Luke!" he exclaimed. "That's beautiful! Just beautiful!" He turned to offer his congratulations to the ghostly tutor who had achieved so much in such a short time, but he was nowhere to be seen.

"Where's Wolfgang?" Mike asked.

Luke paused his playing just long enough to shrug, then went back to creating wonderful music.

"OK," whispered Mike. "Well, keep up the good work!" He stepped back out into the corridor, and quietly closed the door.

"Well?" asked Sue.

Mike nodded enthusiastically. "It's him!" he beamed. "Luke's playing that! Oh, I always knew he was going to be different!"

"He's already different," his wife reminded him. "He's a werewolf."

"No!" cried Mike, barely able to contain his excitement. "He's a werewolf *prodigy*!"

Back in the bedroom, Luke finished the piece with a flourish and jumped up from the stool. His skin began to ripple, and the lights flickered as Wolfgang leapt out of his body. The ghostly composer hung in the air for a moment, then slowly sank down until he was standing on the floor.

"That was unbelievable!" cried Luke.

"Ya," said Wolfgang modestly. "I vould be famous. I'm only a nobody because I have no body. Ha, ha, ha, ha! Did you get zat one?"

Luke was too busy staring down at his fingers to laugh.

"Ah, vell," said Wolfgang. "Now ve just have

to find a vay to make you able to play as well as zat in ze next twenty-four hours."

"Isn't it obvious?" asked Luke with a smile.

Wolfgang looked blank, and a little more transparent than usual. "Nein."

"You could do the exam *for* me, in my body!" exclaimed Luke. "I mean, technically it would still be me. Sort of. Go on, Wolfgang, please?"

The composer stepped back and thought for a second. "Hmmm."

In an effort to persuade him, Luke sat back at the piano and tried to pick out a simple melody. It sounded awful.

"OK, OK!" said Wolfgang urgently. "I vill ze exam do..."

"Yes!" said Luke, with a fist pump.

"...if," continued Wolfgang, "you let me borrow your body to write my second symphony."

Now it was Luke's turn to think. Being possessed by the ghost had been uncomfortable, but not painful. And he did want to do well in the exam and make his parents proud. "Of course!" he said, with a grin. "Absolutely!"

"Deal?" asked Wolfgang.

"Deal!" said Luke, reaching out to shake

his tutor's translucent hand. His fingers went straight through.

When the day of the music exam finally arrived, Dr Skully's pupils talked of little else. Instruments of all shapes and sizes could be heard blasting out all over Scream Street as students fit in one last practice session before heading off to school.

Luke caught up with Resus and Cleo as they walked up to the school's entrance. "Ready for this, chaps?" he asked, throwing his arms around his friends.

"As ready as I'll ever be," said Cleo with a yawn. "I was up all night practising."

"Yeah," said Resus. "That was my plan as well – to stay up all night and prepare for an exam. Except I didn't, because I'm not a bonkers, bandaged brain-box!"

Cleo glared at him. "Just because I take my education seriously..." she began.

"I take mine seriously too!" countered Resus. "Seriously chilled!"

With a huff, Cleo stomped inside the house. Luke and Resus shared a grin.

"Sometimes it's just too easy to wind her up,"

said the vampire.

"You really haven't practised for the exam?" asked Luke.

"Of course I have!" said Resus. "I just wasn't going to tell Cleo that."

Brrrrriiiiiinnnnnnggg!

The boys made their way inside.

"What about you?" Resus asked. "How did your piano tutor work out?"

"It's funny," said Luke, glancing over his shoulder and making sure that Wolfgang was hiding in the bushes as he'd promised. "We really made a connection."

"Right," said Dr Skully when everyone had settled down. "As you know, today is the school music exam." He paused to suck at the end of his pencil. "I have a list of everyone here, and I shall call you out in a random order to perform. You will be given a grade after you have played."

"Cleo thinks he should give out her grade before she even begins," said Resus quietly. Luke chuckled.

"Settle down, everybody," said Dr Skully, his eyes scanning the room from above his spectacles.

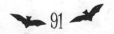

"I think we'll have Dixon first."

Dixon — the mayor's trainee — stood and grabbed a large cello case from the floor.

"Ooh!" said Dr Skully. "Now, this looks promising!"

Dixon dragged it towards the front of the room, banging it into just about everyone on his way.

"Ow!

"Sorry!"

"Oof!"

"Sorry!"

"Dixon!"

"Pardon me!"

Reaching the front, he opened the case — and took out a tiny metal triangle and a stick.

"Oh dear," moaned Dr Skully, putting down his green pen and pulling a red marker from his pocket.

Leaning forward, Dixon studied the sheet of music in front of him, waiting and waiting, until...

Ding!

He played the triangle once, then put it back inside the cello case and took a bow.

Scowling, Dr Skully scribbled an 'E' grade next to Dixon's name.

The rest of the morning passed in much the same manner. Luella produced a trombone from its case, sat on a stool at the front, then waved her hand in the air and danced as the instrument magically played itself.

"I thought we'd talked about this!" scolded Dr Skully, giving out his second 'E' of the day.

Farp the goblin was up next. He strode confidently to the front of the classroom, twirling a trumpet over and over in his fingers. "Be anyone like jazz?" he asked.

"Ooh, I do!" enthused Dr Skully. "I've got a full collection of Buddy Ribs albums, and I'm rather partial to the music of Gooey Armstrong!"

"Then be listen to this!" Farp grinned. He raised the trumpet to his lips, paused, and then spun around. Holding the narrow end of the instrument by his bottom, he began to *fart* into it!

Root-te-toot-toot! Tiddly-tiddly-toot-te-toot!

The entire class ran for the windows and the exit — and fresh air — as clouds of stinking green gas erupted from the other end of the trumpet. Luke pushed the window up as far as it would go, tears streaming from his stinging eyes. He took in a few gulps of air, then turned to find Resus in a similar situation.

"Are your eyes stinging too?" he asked, handing over a tissue.

Resus took it and wiped away his own tears. "No," he said, smacking his palm onto the windowsill again and again. "That's just the funniest thing I've ever seen!"

Once Dr Skully had aired out the classroom and convinced the other pupils it was safe to come back inside, he awarded Farp an 'E' grade and ran a bony finger down his list.

"The next student will be... Oh, thank the sacred bones! Cleo Farr!"

Luke and Resus rolled their eyes as Cleo took a seat at the piano. She began to play a jumpy boogie-woogie tune that soon had everyone tapping their toes and clicking their fingers.

Dr Skully sighed happily, and awarded Cleo an 'A', only marking it down to an 'A−' when the mummy decided to show off and play the second half of the tune with her feet.

"I'd like to see someone beat that!" said Cleo, sitting back at her desk.

"Then listen and weep!" said Resus, sliding an

electric guitar from its case. Luke grinned when he saw the instrument. The body was scarlet red, with orange flames painted around the edges. The neck resembled a long, hissing snake, and the tuning pegs were all pearl fangs.

"Wow!" he breathed.

Now it was Cleo's turn to roll her eyes.

Resus plugged the guitar into his amp, and turned the volume up to 13. Then, grabbing a plectrum shaped like a bat, he began to play the loudest, most aggressive guitar solo Dr Skully had ever heard.

The vampire's fingers ran up and down the neck of the guitar like angry centipedes, hammering down notes and bending the strings to create music that seemed to get inside the head of everyone in the room and make their brains itch.

Doug the zombie appeared outside the window, his jaw having dropped so far that it fell off and clattered to the ground. "Gnarly sounds, little vampire dude!" he proclaimed, clicking his mandible back into place.

"Er, yes, thank you, Resus!" said Dr Skully. But Resus was on his knees, lost in the moment, and he continued to play.

95

"That's enough, Master Negative!" ordered Dr Skully. Still Resus's fingers climbed higher and higher on the neck of the guitar.

"Resus!" bellowed Dr Skully. "Stop that now, before—"

Smash!

Resus stopped, a high wailing note slowly dissipating. He looked up to see that every piece of glass in the classroom had shattered − from the windows to Dr Skully's reading glasses.

"Sorry!" he said, climbing to his feet and taking a bow. "Bit carried away there! Encore?"

Resus also got an 'E'.

Then it was Luke's turn to play.

Chapter Four
THE TRUTH

"Now then, Master Watson," said Dr Skully, retrieving spare glasses from his desk drawer and slipping them on, "the last time I heard you play, it sounded like you'd declared war on music and were taking no prisoners. Shall I just give you an 'E' now and move on, or would you like to torture us first?"

"Actually, sir," said Luke, "I think you'll find my musical abilities have taken quite a spooky turn for the better!"

"Oh, very well," sighed Dr Skully. "Off you go, and do try to leave the piano in one piece this time."

"Yes, sir," said Luke. "I just need to, er, grab my sheet music first. I left it over there, by the window."

Luke dashed to the open window and pretended to root through his school bag for his music. "Wolfgang!" he hissed. "Are you there?"

A shimmering figure appeared in the bushes outside. "Ya," he said. "Here I am, vaiting!"

Luke stretched out his hand. "Then let's do this."

Wolfgang leapt from his hiding place and made contact with Luke's outstretched fingers. Luke experienced the same ice-cold sensation he had felt the last time the ghost possessed him, but this time it was sliding up his arm towards his chest.

After a few seconds, Luke gasped as he felt the composer take over his entire body.

"When you're ready, Master Watson!" said Dr Skully impatiently.

"Ya, ya," said Luke in a German accent. "Oh, I mean yeah, yeah! Keep your hair on, old chap!"

Dr Skully ran a hand over his shiny, white skull and gave out a *harumph*!

Luke sat at the piano and began to play. The classroom fell silent as everyone leaned in to listen to the most wonderful music they had ever heard.

Resus reached over and gently closed Cleo's mouth. "He's not bad, now, is he?" the vampire whispered.

Sobbing with joy, Dr Skully marked an 'A+' next to Luke's name. "Oh, that's beautiful," he sniffed. "Just beautiful!"

Later that afternoon, Luke's and Resus's mums were out in their respective front gardens, tidying up. Sue snipped away the few dead flowers she could find, while Bella did the opposite and got rid of anything that looked fresh, colourful and vibrant.

Suddenly, the gate to number 13 crashed open and Luke raced up the path, closely followed by Wolfgang.

"How did it go?" asked Sue, standing up and brushing the dirt from her knees.

"Yeah, not bad," said Luke, trying to keep a straight face.

But he couldn't maintain the charade for long. "I came top!" he cried.

"You did?" asked Mike, peeking out from behind the front door. "That's brilliant!"

"I'm so proud!" said Sue, giving Luke a hug.

"Wolfgang!" said Mike, finally swinging the door open and stepping outside.

"I always knew you were the man for the job! Come here..."

Mike threw his arms wide and hurried over to the tutor — only to pass straight through him. By the time he emerged at the other side, his smile had disappeared, and his skin had turned a sickly white.

"I think I just touched your intestines!" he croaked.

Slam!

Cleo's father, Niles Farr, jumped as the front door to his house shut with a crash, almost causing him to drop the parchment newspaper he was reading.

"How did it go?" he asked as his daughter stomped across the room.

Slam!

The young mummy's bedroom door got the same treatment.

"That well, eh?" he said to himself.

"Yes!" exclaimed Luke, pacing up and down energetically in his bedroom. "I smashed it! I smashed it!"

He looked up as Wolfgang shimmered into the room. "I mean *we*... We smashed it!"

"Ya," agreed the ghost. "It is now most certainly smashed, vatever zat means. Now, let us not be forgetting your side of ze bargain."

"No problem," said Luke, beaming. "Second symphony. Let's get cracking!" He held his hand out towards the composer. "How long will it take?"

"Vell," said Wolfgang, floating across the room towards Luke. "Ze first one took..." The ghost paused to count on his fingers. "Tventy years."

"Twenty years?" cried Luke, pulling his hand back.

Wolfgang began to laugh. "Ha, ha, ha, ha! You should be seeing your face! I am joking, of course!"

"Phew!" said Luke.

"It was more like nineteen."

Luke opened his mouth to protest, only for Wolfgang to jump right in and possess his body within seconds.

Mike lay in bed with his oversized yellow headphones covering his ears. Beside him, Sue buried her head into her pillow and screamed in frustration.

"Gaaarrrgh!"

Her husband's eyes fluttered open. "No, thanks," he said. "I'm not thirsty."

Glaring, Sue lifted one of the foam-lined domes from her husband's ear. "It's three o'clock in the morning, and Luke is still playing the piano," she grumbled.

Mike turned his head towards the wall. It was true; beautiful snippets of classical music could be heard coming from the room next door. "He's really got into it, hasn't he?"

"I don't care whether or not he's into it any more," she groaned. "I just want to get some sleep!"

Mike smiled kindly. "Well, you should have thought ahead and bought some lovely

102

headphones like mine."

Sue let the earpiece snap back into place with a *slap!*

"Ow!" cried Mike.

"Clumsy me!" said Sue. "Was that your head?"

Mike smiled. "Breakfast in bed?" he said, turning over. "That's very kind of you. See you in the morning!"

Within seconds, he was snoring softly as the piano music continued to drift through the house.

Luke's mum covered her face with the pillow and screamed again.

Moonlight streamed in through the window as Luke sat at the piano, his eyes drooping while his fingers raced up and down the keys. He desperately wanted to sleep. But now that Wolfgang had a body for the first time in centuries, he wasn't going to take a break any time soon.

Snatching up a pencil, Wolfgang scribbled out the line of music he'd just created, then tried out a slight variation. To Luke's ears they sounded exactly the same — but then again, he didn't have control of them.

"Ach! Nein, nein, nein!" Wolfgang muttered,

screwing up the sheet of music and tossing it onto the floor to join a small mountain of wasted paper.

A bat screeched outside the window as the composer used Luke's fingers to grab a fresh sheet, and then they started composing once more...

"It's weird, if you ask me," said Resus, staring up at Luke's bedroom window a few hours later. He was standing in the street with Cleo and Dig, listening to the piano music. "When has Luke ever spent all night in his room working?"

Cleo huffed. "When have I ever come second?" she asked. "Something is wrong. Very wrong."

"Come on," said Resus. "Let's get to the bottom of this."

Sue let Luke's friends into the house with a yawn and ushered them upstairs before heading to the kitchen for her third cup of coffee.

Resus barged into Luke's room without knocking, Cleo at his heels. "Hey, Luke!" he said, jovially. "We just popped in to see if everything is all right."

Luke didn't look up from the piano. "Ya, ya!" he said, in Wolfgang's thick accent. "Everything is A-okey-dokey!"

Resus and Cleo shared a worried glance, just as Dig pushed past them to sniff at Luke's feet, which were working hard at the piano's pedals. The half-hound looked up and began to growl.

"Aaarrrgh!" screamed Wolfgang, leaping out of Luke's skin and backing away in the air.

Luke's head dropped instantly, and he began to snore.

"What's going on?" demanded Cleo.

But Wolfgang was too terrified to answer. "Get it out!" he yelled, trembling. "Get it out!"

Resus grabbed a balled-up piece of music from the floor and tossed it out into the hallway. "Go, boy," he said. "Fetch!"

Dig chased after the bull, and Resus closed the door behind him.

"Zank you!" said Wolfgang, floating down to the floor. "I have ze phobia for doggies. I get it from mein papa. He vas a postman, not a famous composer like me."

"Composer?" said Cleo. She grabbed Luke's shoulder and shook him awake. "You mean this is your piano tutor?"

"Huh?" Luke rubbed his eyes.

"What's the *inside* story, Luke?"

Luke sighed. "All right," he groaned. "So, Wolfgang did my music exam for me."

"I knew it!" Cleo cried.

"Ah, but you did not know zat Luke and I make ze deal, little wrapped-up girl und pointy-toothed boy!" snapped Wolfgang. "Now, buzzing off, you will be!"

Luke shrugged at his friends as the composer dived back inside his body. Pausing only to blow Resus and Cleo a raspberry, Wolfgang turned back to the piano keys and continued to play.

"But..." said Cleo.

"Out!" yelled Wolfgang. "Sob, sob, sad violins!"

"Come on," sighed Resus, leading Cleo out of the bedroom.

As the pair made for the stairs, the telephone began to ring. Mike hurried out of the living room to answer it. "Hello?"

"Mr Watson!" said the voice at the other end of the line. "Dr Skully here. I have some simply tremendous news..."

Moments later, Mike was pushing his way past Resus, Cleo and Dig as he dashed up to Luke's bedroom. He flung the door open and announced, "You're going to be headlining at the school concert!" before racing downstairs again to find his wife.

As soon as the door closed, Wolfgang leapt from Luke's body again and began to skip in circles around the room. "I vill perform in front of a real audience again! Yahoo!"

Luke stood up from the piano stool. He felt exhausted. "Listen, Wolfgang," he said. "I've been thinking about our deal. I mean, it isn't exactly fair."

"Nein!" snapped the composer, glaring down at Luke. "Ze symphony is not yet finished! Break ze deal, und I vill tell your fazerpapa. He will so disappointed be."

Luke shrugged. "It won't be the first time."

"OK," said Wolfgang, calming down. "Fair enough. In zese circumstances, zare is only one sensible thing to do."

"And what's that?" asked Luke.

The composer closed in on him. "I shall not leave your body ever again!"

Chapter Five

THE CONCERT

The following day, Dr Skully enlisted the help of the Movers, Scream Street's faceless security men, to build a bandstand in the central square. Across the top hung a banner that read: 'School concert, featuring piano prodigy Luke Watson'.

Resus and Cleo watched as Scream Street's residents filled row after row of seats.

"Luke's really lost it this time," sighed Resus.

The audience chatter fell away as Dr Skully took to the stage and approached the microphone.

"In all my years of teaching, I always knew I would find a genius, one day..."

"You have," muttered Cleo under her breath. "Me!"

Dr Skully continued. "But nothing could have prepared me for the utter joy I felt when I heard this next student play. Ladies and gentlemen, Master Luke Watson!"

Applause filled the central square as Luke took to the stage. Thanks to the eagerness of Wolfgang inside him, he strode confidently to the piano, took a deep bow and sat down at the keyboard.

"I can't wait to see that imposter's face when he finds our little surprise!" hissed Cleo.

Resus giggled. "It's certainly going to be a showstopper!"

Silence fell on the square as Luke began to play. The music – an early draft of Wolfgang's second symphony – was more beautiful than ever. Dr Skully whipped out a handkerchief and dabbed at his eyes. Mike and Sue held hands and sighed happily as their son gave the performance of a lifetime. Even Farp stopped farting long enough to listen. Then...

Clunk!

Luke hit a wrong note. The audience gasped. Dr Skully looked up. Farp trumped.

"I am, as you say, sorry!" said Luke. "I shall try zat again."

He backed up a few bars and began to play again. Then...

Clunk!

Luke hit the dud key repeatedly.

Clunk! Clunk! Clunk!

"Hmmm... Zare is definitely somezing not right viz zat key." Luke stood and opened the piano lid to investigate...

...to find Dig hiding inside the instrument, growling back at him!

Woof!

The ghost of Wolfgang von Mozhoven screamed and leapt out of Luke's body in an effort to escape.

The audience gasped – everyone but Resus and Cleo, who were busy high-fiving each other. Their plan had worked!

Dig jumped out of the piano and closed in on Wolfgang.

"Nice doggie!" the composer croaked. The only safe place was back inside the boy. The ghost started forward, then froze when he saw Luke's expression of rage.

"Stay out of my body!" Luke snarled. Then he threw back his head and let loose a strangled cry. A familiar black shadow enveloped him as his werewolf transformation began.

Still in their seats, Resus and Cleo watched in horror. Their plan had backfired. "Luke's changing!" Resus gulped.

"In the middle of a packed square!" added Cleo.

The pair jumped up and began to force their way through the spectators towards their friend.

Up on the stage, Luke screamed in agony as his face reshaped; a long snout stretched forward and sharp teeth emerged from his gums. His spine broke and reformed, now twisted and thick. Yellow talons ripped their way through his fingertips, and fur sprouted over every inch of his body. His tail appeared and ears rose up to complete the transformation.

"Hooooowwwwwwwwllllllll!"

An eerie quiet fell over the crowd in the central square. Then one lone voice near the back said, matter-of-factly, "I say – that's a werewolf!"

 111

Then the panic started.

Monsters of all shapes and sizes screamed and ran for safety. Bog beasts slimed over fallen vampires, zombies lost body parts as they battled past witches, and goblins used their farts to propel themselves over the heads of mummies to escape.

As Resus and Cleo dashed past Doug, the zombie's legs made a break for it, leaving the top half of the rotten reveler lying on the ground. "Guys!" he yelled after them. "Wait up!"

Cleo reached the stage first and reached out to the wolf. "Luke!" she cried. "You have to stop this! You have to change back!"

But the wolf was far too busy searching for Wolfgang. Its bright yellow eyes spotted the composer hurrying away, and it gave chase with a snarl. The composer heard the noise and looked back to see the werewolf in pursuit. He squealed and turned to the nearest person in the crowd, witch Eefa Everwell.

"Don't you even think about—" barked Eefa.

But before she could finish the sentence, Wolfgang jumped off the stage and took over her body. The wolf was on the combined pair in a second, sniffing up and down the witch's long, red dress.

Terrified, Wolfgang jumped out of Eefa, landing inside the body of the mayor's personal Mover, NoName.

"Huh?" The faceless bodyguard reached up to scratch his head, then turned to face its master.

"What's the matter with you?" demanded the mayor, Sir Otto Sneer.

Snarl!

Sneer felt the wolf's hot breath on the back of his neck, and fainted. NoName caught his boss, forcing Wolfgang to vacate his body and run even further into the terrified crowd.

Across the square, Cleo stopped chasing Luke's werewolf and paused to catch her breath. "This is useless!" she gasped.

"I know," agreed Resus. "But we have to try to stop him! It's not like you to give up."

Cleo winked at her friend. "Who says I'm giving up? Come on, this way!" And with that, she led Resus away from the wolf and back towards the stage.

Wolfgang floated away as fast as he could,

trying to dodge his way between the monsters around him.

"*Hooooowwwwwwwwwwlllllllll!*"

The ghostly composer looked over his shoulder towards the sound. When he turned back, he found himself accidentally taking over yet another body – this time, it was Mike's.

The werewolf pounced, sending Luke's father crashing to the ground. It snarled, long tendrils of warm drool dripping onto Mike's face.

"L-Luke!" Wolfgang stammered through Mike's mouth as he gazed up at the monster above him. "Zis is your papa! You vouldn't be hurting your own papafazer now, vould you?"

But Luke was too far down inside the wolf to listen to reason. With a final growl, the creature prepared to bite...

Wolfgang screamed. "Eeeeeeeeeeeeek!"

"Yee-hah!" came a cry from across the square. The wolf paused in its attack to look up. It saw Cleo standing in the middle of the street. She had tied a length of bandage to the school tuba and was swinging it around her head like an Olympic hammer-thrower.

After a few spins, she let go of the bandage

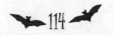

and watched as the heavy brass instrument flew through the air. It landed with a satisfying *thunk* right over the werewolf's head.

The wolf leapt up, shaking its head to try to dislodge the instrument, but it was stuck tight.

Wolfgang took the opportunity to scramble out of Mike's body and away from danger. Until...

"Oi, Wiggy ghosty!" shouted Resus. "I've got your music!"

"Nein!" cried Wolfgang at the sight of the vampire clutching a handful of handwritten pages. "Mein precious second symphony!" He began to move towards Resus.

The vampire made a tiny tear in the pages. "Stay back," he warned. "I'll do it!"

"You vouldn't dare," spat the composer, taking a step forward.

"Oh, yes I vould," growled Resus, tearing just a little bit more of the music.

Cleo looked from Wolfgang to Resus and back as the stand-off continued. She heard a groan behind her and turned to see a now-human Luke emerging from beneath the tuba. She hurried over to help him.

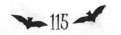

"You don't want to miss this!" she promised.

"Eefa," called Resus, holding Wolfgang's music up in the air. "Would you mind getting rid of this rubbish?"

The witch climbed up onto the stage to join Resus. "My pleasure," she said.

Before Wolfgang could react, Resus tossed the symphony up into the air. Eefa blew across her hand to create a magical gale that lifted and carried the sheets away, dancing on the wind.

Wolfgang von Mozhoven gave chase, closely followed by Dig, who jumped up repeatedly, teeth snapping at the composer's transparent tushie.

"Nein! Nein! Mein beautiful music!" screeched Wolfgang as he ran off into the distance after the greatest work of his death. "You philistines! Nice doggie! Argh! Mein symphony! Sob, sob, sad violins!"

Mike and Sue lay in bed that evening, listening to Luke hammer out one awful tune after another on his piano. On the floor beside the bed, Dig slept calmly, a pair of large yellow headphones covering his ears.

"That's it!" said Mike, jumping out of bed as

Luke began another dreadful ditty. "I'm going to say something."

Seconds later, he flung open Luke's bedroom door. "Luke!" he said. "Your piano playing is terrible." He grinned. "And that's just how I like it!"

**AN EXCERPT FROM THE
NEW BOOK IN THE SERIES**

Chapter One
THE GAME

Thick plumes of mist tumbled through the grave-yard, spilling over tombstones like waves crashing onto the rocks of a shoreline. And from the dense fog came the sound of groaning, and shuffling, and the grinding of teeth.

A boy and girl stood in a small clearing between the graves, watching and waiting. They clenched their fists and shifted lightly from foot to foot, ready to pounce as soon as the battle began. Their faces showed no emotion whatsoever.

The first zombie emerged from the mist. Ragged clothes clung to its skeleton-thin frame, which was wrapped in what must once have been human skin. Now it resembled torn leather.

The creature snarled, causing a gush of sticky, scarlet blood to ooze from the missing side of its face. The hole ran from just below its right eye, down through an entirely missing cheek to end at the side of its mouth. Its lips flapped like pieces of wet rubber with every shuffling step.

The undead wretch caught sight of the waiting kids and limped as quickly as it could towards them, just as the rest of the zombie horde emerged from the cascading clouds of mist. Some of them, like the leader of the pack, were almost completely whole. Others had missing limbs, or unseeing eyeballs dangling from veins out of hollow sockets – even exposed sections of brain. But whatever their condition, the entire troop now had the youngsters' scent in their rotting nostrils, and they rushed to attack.

As half-face drew near, the girl leapt into the air, spinning impossibly as wispy tendrils of fog radiated out from her body. Her foot connected with the still-present side of the zombie's face, and the creature's head jerked back. Its decomposing spinal cord snapped with an audible *crack*, and the monster's head was sent flying off to land in the disturbed earth of an anonymous grave.

The zombie sank to its knees. A scream rang out and a digitized number *3,000* appeared, floating above the off-white stump of neck bone. The creature moaned, flickered in and out of view for a second, and then disappeared.

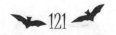

"Yes!" cried a distant voice. "Beat that, Watson!"

As the girl landed lightly, another of the walking dead lunged towards the boy at her side, its mouth open to reveal a severed tongue swarming with maggots. The lifeless beast bore down to bite. The boy stood his ground, then punched straight ahead with his fist, shattering the zombie's ribs. In one swift movement, he grasped the monster's blackened, unbeating heart in his fingers and squeezed until it burst.

Another scream sounded, and a score of *2,000* points appeared as the zombie strobed and vanished.

"What?" exclaimed another disconnected voice. "That move was worth way more than a measly 2,000 points!"

In the living room of 13 Scream Street, Egyptian mummy Cleo Farr stuck out her tongue at her friend, Luke Watson. "You're just mad because you're being beaten by a girl!"

"That's not true!" said Luke. "I mean, I may be losing to a girl at the moment, but I'll obviously win in the end."

"Is that so?"

"Yes, it is completely so!"

Cleo gripped her game controller and turned back to the high-resolution image on the screen. The rest of the computerized zombies were almost within grabbing distance of the characters.

"Let's do this!" she said, cracking her neck from side to side.

The two friends leapt into action, swinging controllers and pressing buttons to send their on-screen avatars into a fighting frenzy. Before long, zombie body parts were flying through the air.

"That one's yours!" yelled Luke as his character put an end to the rampage of yet another grave escapee. A second drooling creature was waiting behind it, ready to pounce.

"Got it!" hissed Cleo, flicking her thumbsticks in a figure-eight shape. Her character executed a perfect spin kick, decapitating her lifeless attacker.

"Kapow!" she shouted as a score of *4,000* points flashed. "So long, ugly!"

Luke's fists pumped as his character pummelled the next in the advancing horde, earning himself a series of *1,000* points in rapid succession, followed by a bright green *10,000* as his opponent crumbled to dust.

"Bonus!" he cried. "What a game! You've got to love *Zombie Kick Boxer*!"

"Actually, dude… I'm finding it kinda offensive."

Luke turned to the third occupant of the room. Sitting in the armchair behind him and Cleo was a figure with lank hair, rotting skin and a set of yellowing, broken teeth.

"Really, Doug?" asked Luke, surprised. "How can this be offensive?"

"Not all zombies are like that, bro," Doug explained. "Some of us, Yours Truly included, prefer chilling to killing."

"Oh," said Luke, his cheeks flushing red. "I didn't think of it that way. This game was huge back in the normal world and, to be fair, I never thought I'd ever play it in front of an actual zombie. Sorry!"

"No problemo, dude," said Doug with a grin. "It's just that those of us who are, you know, 'not quite dead' never get a good rap in those games."

"I suppose not," said Luke.

"And watching you beat up on my brain-dead bros is dredging up some painful memories from the back of my mind." The zombie paused to scratch at his scalp. "At least, I *think* they're memories. It could just be beetles again."

"Er, a little help over here!" With Luke's character paused, Cleo was having to work harder than ever to defeat the tsunami of rotting corpses as they attacked. Her arms and legs flailed around as she took on the ever-growing tide of breathless biters.

"Whoa!" Luke exclaimed, jumping back into the game as his character disappeared beneath three hungry monsters.

"Hurry!" cried Cleo. "You're— Oh, no!"

It was too late. Luke's lifeline at the top of the screen dropped lower and lower as his pixelated persona was chomped upon, slashed and gradually torn apart.

The words "GAME OVER" flashed in the centre of the screen.

"Ha!" beamed Doug, jumping to his feet. "You're dead, bro! Hope you come back as a zombie, then you could see this stuff from my perspective. We could totally hang out!"

Luke grinned. "So long as my dad's not around."

"I hear you, wolfy dude," said Doug, making for the living-room door. "Your old man is still a little wary of us grave-dodgers. I get it. I'll catch you on the flip side."

Just as Doug reached out for the handle, the door swung open and Luke's dad strode into the room. At the sight of the zombie, he squealed, dropped his mug of tea and fell against the window frame.

"Sorry, Mr W!" said Doug. "Didn't mean to scare you!"

"Th-that's OK, D-Doug," whimpered Mike Watson from halfway behind the curtain. "I'm still finding the undead a little hard to get used to!" He began to edge around the walking corpse to his armchair. Then his face paled.

"Yours, I believe," Mike said, plucking a wriggling worm from the back of the chair and handing it over."

"Wilfred!" exclaimed Doug, taking the worm and stuffing it back into his hair as he left the room. "Thanks, man!"

Mike slumped into his chair and tried to calm his breathing.

"You OK, Dad?" Luke asked.

"Never better!" Mike lied. "What are you two kids up to?"

Luke glanced over his shoulder at the zombie carnage on-screen and quickly flicked off his games console. "Not a lot!" he said, smiling. "Why don't you settle back and watch the news while Cleo and I clean up and make you another cup of tea?"

"Well, that sounds very pleasant indeed," said Mike. "Thank you!"

"Any time, Mr Watson!" said Cleo. She switched channels, then picked up the empty mug from the carpet and followed Luke towards the kitchen.

Mike turned his attention to the screen, where he found himself faced with yet another zombie. This one, however, was merely reading the weather report, so Mike was able to keep his terror in check. At least, a little.

"…and this south-westerly breeze should blow the cursed fog safely away from Scream Street by the end of the week," announced Mitch Flesh, the ragged reporter.

"Thank goodness for that!" said Mike to himself.

The weatherman grinned. "Back to you, Anna!" Then he reached up and tore off his own head, replacing it with that of the female newscaster, Anna Gored.

Mike swallowed hard.

"Thanks Mitch," said the new presenter, snapping her head into place with a loud *click*. "Now, exciting news for music fans. Due to the fog mentioned in the weather report, vehicles are unable to enter or leave Scream Street for the time being. This includes tour buses. As a result, top flesh-metal band Brain Drain have been forced to abandon their tour. They will play the remainder of their concerts here in Scream Street."

Luke and Cleo appeared in the doorway.

"Brain Drain!" cried Luke.

"We've got to tell Resus!" exclaimed Cleo.

The pair raced for the front door, slamming it behind them as they hurried out.

Mike sat silently in his chair for a moment, then said, "Er, hello? What happened to my cup of tea?"